Alice in Wonderland

Lewis Carroll
Adapted by Lesley Sims

Illustrated by
Mauro Evangelista

Reading Consultant: Alison Kelly
Roehampton University

Contents

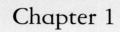

Chapter 1

Down the rabbit hole

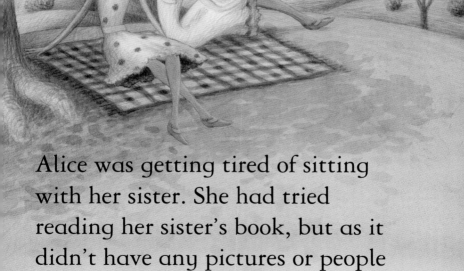

Alice was getting tired of sitting
with her sister. She had tried
reading her sister's book, but as it
didn't have any pictures or people
talking, it was very dull indeed.

She was just wondering whether to pick some daisies for a daisy-chain when a White Rabbit ran past. Now, seeing a rabbit isn't so very remarkable.

Alice wasn't even surprised when the Rabbit cried, "Oh dear! Oh dear! I shall be too late." But when it took a watch out of its pocket, she jumped up. For whoever saw a rabbit with a pocket – or a watch?

She chased after it and was just in time to see the Rabbit pop down a large hole. In a flash, Alice followed.

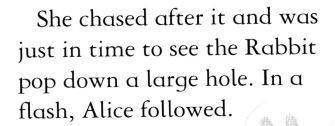

At first, the hole went on like a tunnel. Suddenly, it dipped and Alice found herself falling down a deep well.

The well was lined with shelves full of interesting things – and either it was very deep, or Alice fell slowly, for she had plenty of time to look around.

"I must be near the middle of the earth," she thought, after a while. "What if I fall right through? I might end up in New Zealand!"

Down,
   down,
     down...
Alice began to think the fall
would never end. She was
daydreaming about
her cat, Dinah,
when *thump!* she
landed on a
heap of dry
leaves.

Not in the least hurt, Alice stood up and looked around. A long passage stretched ahead of her and the White Rabbit was hurrying down it. Alice went after him like the wind.

Oh my ears and whiskers, how late it's getting!

She had almost caught up with him when he turned a corner... and vanished.

Alice was in a long hall, with doors down both sides. Excitedly, she tried each one. But every single door was locked.

Just as she thought she might never get out, she saw a glass table with a golden key on top.

Alice walked down the hall once more, but the key was too small for the doors. Then she spotted a tiny door, half-hidden by a curtain. Holding her breath, she tried the golden key in the lock. It worked!

Beyond the door was the most beautiful garden Alice had ever seen, with bright flowers and cool, sparkling fountains. Alice tried to squeeze through the door, but not even her head would fit.

If only I could shrink...

"I'll go back to the table," she decided. "Perhaps it has another key to a bigger door."

But instead of a key, she found a bottle with a label saying *Drink me.* "That wasn't here before," thought Alice, checking it carefully. Since it wasn't marked *Poison*, she took a sip.

It tasted so delicious (a mix of cherry-tart, custard, toffee, pineapple and hot buttered toast), that she had very soon finished it.

"What a curious feeling," Alice said next. "I think I'm shrinking!" And she was. Soon, she was small enough to go into the garden.

I hope I don't shrink away to nothing...

To her huge disappointment, the garden door had closed – and she'd left the golden key on the table. She could see it glittering through the glass, a long way out of reach.

Alice tried to climb a table leg, but it was too slippery. After three tries, she fell to the floor and began to cry. "That won't help," she told herself sharply. As she wiped her eyes, she noticed a glass box under the table.

Eat me

The box held a cake. "I'll eat it," thought Alice. "If I grow larger, I can reach the key. If I grow smaller, I can creep under the door. Either way, I'll get into the garden."

Chapter 2

The pool of tears

"Curiouser and curiouser!" cried Alice, who was suddenly growing at an incredible rate. "Goodbye feet!" She had looked down. Her feet were almost out of sight.

She only stopped growing when her head hit the ceiling. Quickly, she grabbed the key and hurried to the door. Now she was far too big.

Alice began to cry again, sobbing and sobbing until a pool of tears spread around her.

After a while, she heard pattering feet and dried her eyes. It was the White Rabbit, trotting along in a great hurry, and carrying a pair of gloves and a fan.

15

"If you please, Sir," Alice began. The Rabbit jumped in the air and scurried away, dropping the gloves and fan as he went.

Alice picked them up and began to fan herself. "How very strange everything is today!" she thought.

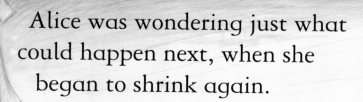

Alice was wondering just what could happen next, when she began to shrink again.

16

Moments before she shrank away altogether, she realized the fan was to blame and dropped it.

"That was a narrow escape," she sighed. "Now for the garden!" But the tiny door had closed and the golden key was back on the table.

Things were worse than ever. Just then, her foot slipped and *splash!* she was up to her chin in salty water.

She'd fallen into her pool of tears. Something else was splashing around too. At first, Alice thought it was a walrus or a hippo. Then she remembered how small she was and saw it was only a mouse.

I wish I hadn't cried so much!

The pool was soon crowded with creatures that had fallen in. Alice led the way and the whole group swam to shore.

Chapter 3

A caucus race

It was a very odd party that gathered on the bank, and all of them were dripping wet, cross and uncomfortable. The first question, of course, was how to get dry.

"The best thing," said a Dodo, "would be a caucus race."

"A *what* race?" asked Alice.

"The best way to explain is to do it," the Dodo replied. There was no "One, two, three, go!" Everyone began and ended when they liked. After about half an hour, the Dodo called out, "It's over!" and they all crowded around, asking who won.

They surrounded Alice,
demanding prizes. In despair, she
felt in her pocket and pulled out
a tin of peppermints. There were
enough for exactly one each.

"But she must have a prize
too," said the Mouse.

"Of course," said the
Dodo. "What else is
in your pocket?"

Alice took out a
thimble and the Dodo
solemnly presented
it to her.

Then they sat down in a circle.
The Mouse started to tell them a
story, but he left in a huff when he
thought Alice wasn't listening.

"I wish Dinah was here," said
Alice. "She'd soon bring him back."

"Who's Dinah?" asked a bird.

"Our cat," Alice said eagerly
and, in no time at
all, the creatures
had gone.

Chapter 4

The White Rabbit's house

As the creatures left, the long hall vanished and the White Rabbit appeared. "Mary Ann!" he snapped, when he saw Alice. "Run home and fetch me some gloves and a fan."

"He thinks I'm his maid!" Alice thought, but she ran off in the direction he pointed. Soon, she came to a small house with *W. Rabbit* on a brass plate outside.

Racing in, she found a fan and some gloves on a table.

Alice was about to leave, when she saw a bottle. This one had no label but she drank it anyway. *Something* interesting was bound to happen...

And it did. She had barely drunk
half, before she grew as big as the
room. She went on growing... and
growing... until one arm was out of
the window and her foot was stuck
up the chimney.

"Mary Ann!" called the Rabbit, crossly. "Where are my gloves?"

Alice trembled, quite forgetting she was now a thousand times larger than him and had no reason to be scared.

When he couldn't open the door — because Alice's elbow was against it — he tried the window. Alice waved her hand and heard a shriek.

26

"Pat! Where
are you?"
the Rabbit
shouted and
Alice heard a
new voice reply,
"Over here sir."
"Well, tell me," asked
the Rabbit, "what's
in this window?"
"An arm, sir,"
said the voice.

"An arm, you goose!" said
the Rabbit. "Whoever saw
one that size? Take it away!"

The next thing Alice knew, the
Rabbit had yelled, "Bill! Go down
the chimney."

Alice waited until she
heard a little animal
scrabbling inside the
chimney and gave
a sharp kick.

We must burn the
house down.

Don't you
dare!

There goes Bill.

There was silence for a moment,
then a shower of pebbles came
rattling through the window.
To Alice's surprise, they turned
into cakes.

"If I eat them," she thought,
"they're bound to change my size.
And as I can't grow any larger, I
expect I'll grow smaller."

Alice shrank at once. As soon as she could squeeze through the door, she fled. And she didn't stop running until she reached a forest.

"The first thing I have to do," she decided when she had caught her breath, "is to grow to my right size. Then I must find a way into that lovely garden."

It was an excellent plan. The
only problem was how to do it. "I
suppose I should eat or drink
something," she said.
"But what?"

Alice looked around and saw a
mushroom. Standing on tiptoe, she
peered over the edge to see a
large caterpillar, quietly minding
its own business.

Chapter 5

The Caterpillar's advice

The Caterpillar and Alice looked at each other for a while.

"Who are *you*?" the Caterpillar asked finally, in a sleepy voice.

"I- I hardly know, sir," said Alice.

"What do you mean?" demanded the Caterpillar. "Explain yourself!"

"Try reciting a poem," ordered the Caterpillar. Clearing her throat, Alice began.

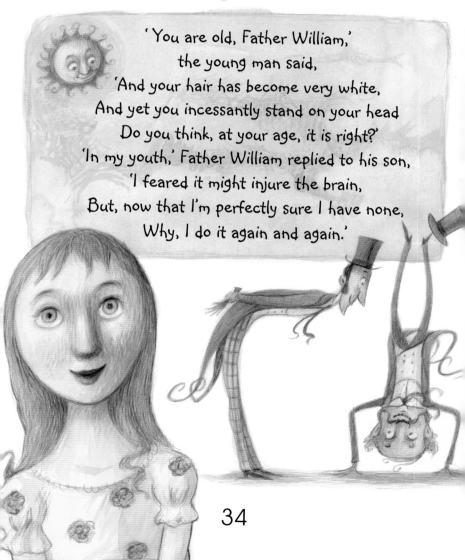

'You are old, Father William,'
the young man said,
'And your hair has become very white,
And yet you incessantly stand on your head
Do you think, at your age, it is right?'
'In my youth,' Father William replied to his son,
'I feared it might injure the brain,
But, now that I'm perfectly sure I have none,
Why, I do it again and again.'

"Wrong from beginning to end!" said the Caterpillar. He paused. "What size do you want to be?"

"Larger than this," said Alice.

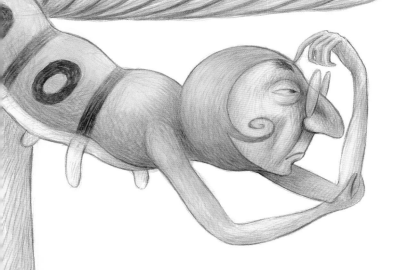

"It's such a wretched height."

"It's a very good height indeed," said the Caterpillar (who was exactly as tall as Alice). He slid off the mushroom angrily.

"One side makes you taller, the other makes you shorter," he remarked, as he crawled away.

"One side of *what*?" wondered Alice. "Oh, the mushroom!" She broke off two pieces and nibbled first one, then the other, until she was back to her right size.

Alice continued through the forest until she came to a little house. "I don't want to scare anyone," she thought and ate some more mushroom to shrink herself.

Chapter 6

Pig and pepper

As Alice looked at the house, a fish dressed as a footman ran up and rapped wetly on the door. It was opened by a frog. Alice crept closer.

They bowed low and their wigs got tangled. Alice laughed so loudly, she had to run back into the trees. When she came out, the fish had gone.

I shall sit here till tomorrow... or the next day.

Timidly, Alice went up to the door and knocked. "There's no use knocking," said the Frog. "I'm on the same side as you. Besides, they're making too much noise to hear."

"How will I get in?" asked Alice.

"Are you to get in at all?" said the Frog. "That's the question."

"Hopeless!" thought Alice and marched straight into a large kitchen. A grumpy Duchess sat in the middle holding a baby, a cat at her feet. Pepper filled the air.

Alice sneezed. "Why is your cat grinning?" she asked the Duchess.

"It's a Cheshire cat," the Duchess replied briskly.

"I didn't know cats *could* grin," Alice said.

"They all can," said the Duchess, "and most of 'em do."

"I don't know any that do," said Alice.

"You don't know much and that's a fact."

All of a sudden, the Cook began throwing pans at the Duchess, who simply ignored her and sang a lullaby to the howling baby.

Speak roughly
to your little boy
And beat him
when he sneezes
He only does it to annoy
Because he knows
it teases.

"Here!" she finished suddenly, flinging the baby at Alice. "You look after it. I must get ready for the Queen."

41

Alice caught the baby and left before they were hit by a flying frying-pan. The baby grunted and Alice glanced down. To her surprise, it was turning into a pig.

"Oh!" she cried and let it go. Alice was thinking it was more handsome as a pig, when she saw the Cheshire Cat grinning at her.

"Cheshire Cat," she said, shyly, "where should I go now?"

"Well, that way is a Hatter," said the Cat, waving a paw, "and *that* way is a March Hare. Both mad."

"But I don't want to visit mad people," Alice said.

"We're all mad here," said the Cat, fading away.

Chapter 7

A mad tea party

"As it's May, the March Hare might not be quite so mad," Alice thought and decided to visit him. The March Hare was sitting in front of his house having tea with the Hatter.

"No room! No room!" they cried
when they saw Alice.

"There's plenty of room!" she
said indignantly, sitting down.

The Hatter stared at Alice.
"Why is a raven like a writing
desk?" he demanded.

Then he took out his watch and
shook it. "Two days wrong," he
complained.

He sighed and turned to Alice.
"Have you guessed the riddle yet?"
"I give up," she said. "What is it?"
The Hatter shrugged. "No idea."
"You shouldn't waste time asking
riddles with no answer," she snapped.

"Oh, time and I aren't speaking," said the Hatter. "We argued at a concert given by the Queen of Hearts. I sang a song, you know."

Twinkle, twinkle, little bat!
How I wonder what you're at!
Up above the world you fly
Like a tea-tray in the sky...

"I'd hardly finished the first verse," he went on, "when the Queen shouted I was murdering time. It's been tea time ever since."

"I'm bored," the March Hare interrupted. "I want a story." And he pinched a large Dormouse, who was dozing beside them.

Once upon a time, three girls lived down a treacle well...

"This is the stupidest tea party ever!" thought Alice and walked off.

48

Back in the forest, she noticed a
tree with a door in the trunk.
Curious, she stepped inside...

The tree led her back to the long
hall and, this time, the door behind
the curtain was open. At last, she
could enter the beautiful garden.

Chapter 8

Meeting the Queen

At the garden's entrance was a tree covered with white roses, which three gardeners were busily painting red.

Before Alice could ask what they were doing, one of them called out, "The Queen!" and all three threw themselves flat on their faces. Alice looked around, eager to see her.

"Who are *these*?" the Queen
barked, spotting the gardeners.

"How should *I* know?" said Alice.

"Off with her head!" screamed
the Queen.

"Nonsense!" Alice said, firmly.
The Queen looked at the rose tree
and turned to the gardeners.

"Off with *their* heads!"

Quickly, Alice threw
the gardeners
into a pot.

"Come and play croquet," the Queen shouted at Alice next.

Alice had never played such a strange game.

Everyone played at once and the Queen stomped about shouting, "Off with their heads!"

Alice was wondering if she could escape when she saw a grin.

"How are you getting along?" asked the Cheshire Cat, as soon as its mouth was all there.

Alice waited for its ears before replying. "They don't follow any rules," she complained, "and as for the Queen..."

"...she's too good," Alice finished quickly, as the Queen walked by.

"Off with his head," the Queen snapped at the Cat.

Instantly, the Cat's body vanished.

"I can't cut off a head if there's no body to cut it from," declared the executioner.

"Anything with a head can be beheaded," the King argued.

"Everyone will lose their heads in a minute," said the Queen and sent for the Duchess to sort out her Cat.

The game went on until the
Queen's soldiers had arrested
almost everyone. While the King
was letting them go again,
someone suddenly shouted.

"Time for the trial!"

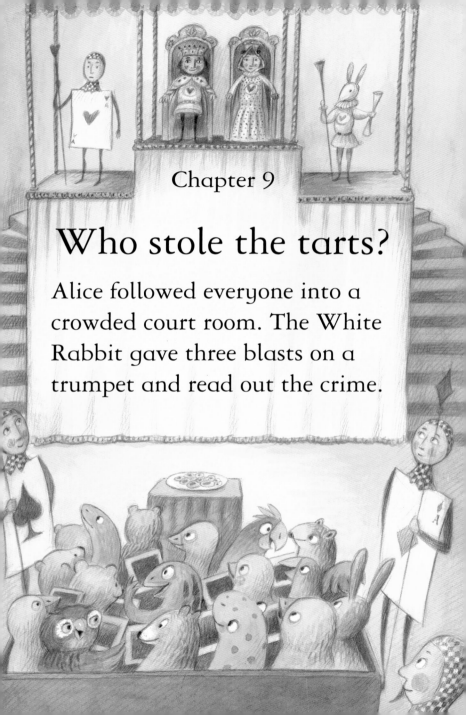

Chapter 9

Who stole the tarts?

Alice followed everyone into a crowded court room. The White Rabbit gave three blasts on a trumpet and read out the crime.

The Queen of Hearts, she made some tarts
All on a summer day
The Knave of Hearts, he stole those tarts
And took them quite away!

"Consider your verdict," the King ordered the jury.

"Not yet!" cried the Rabbit. "Call the first witness!"

This was the Hatter, who walked in trembling. He was shaking so much, both his shoes fell off.

As Alice watched, she felt an odd sensation. She was growing larger.

"He's useless!" said the King and sent the Hatter away. "Next!"

The Duchess's Cook came in.

The Cook annoyed the King even more. "Who's next?" he shouted.

Alice wanted to know too. The witnesses so far had been terrible. Imagine her surprise when the White Rabbit called out, "Alice!"

Chapter 10

Alice's evidence

"Here!" Alice cried, jumping up. But she'd grown so big, she sent the jury box flying and everyone fell out.

"What do you know about all this?" demanded the King.

"Nothing," said Alice.

"Let the jury consider their verdict," the King announced.

"Sentence first, verdict later," insisted the Queen.

By now, Alice had grown to her
full size. "You're nothing but a
pack of cards!" she scoffed. At this,
the whole pack rose into the air
and came flying down upon her.

Alice screamed... and woke up to find her sister gently brushing dead leaves from her face. "Oh, I've had such a wonderful dream," she said and told her all about it, before running off for tea.

Lewis Carroll (1832-1898)

Lewis Carroll was the made-up name of Charles Lutwidge Dodgson, a vicar and teacher. He first told the story *Alice's Adventures Underground* to amuse his young friend, Alice Liddell, during a boat trip. She asked him to write it down and in 1865 it was published with the title *Alice's Adventures in Wonderland*. A sequel, *Through the Looking-Glass, and What Alice Found There*, was published six years later.

Designed by Katarina Dragoslavic

Cover design by Russell Punter

First published in 2006 by Usborne Publishing Ltd., Usborne House, 83-85 Saffron Hill, London EC1N 8RT, England. www.usborne.com
Copyright © 2006 Usborne Publishing Ltd.